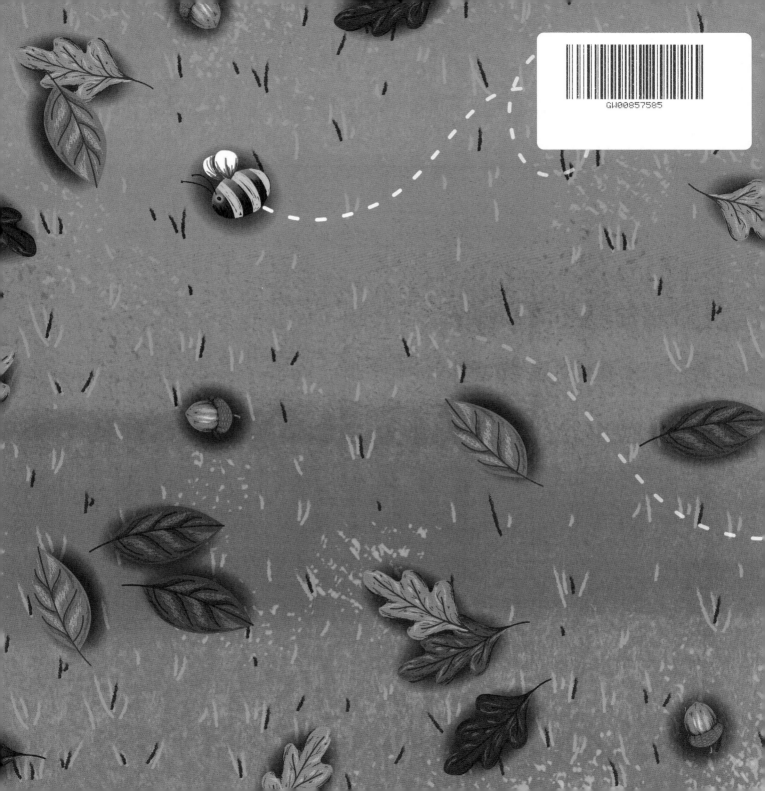

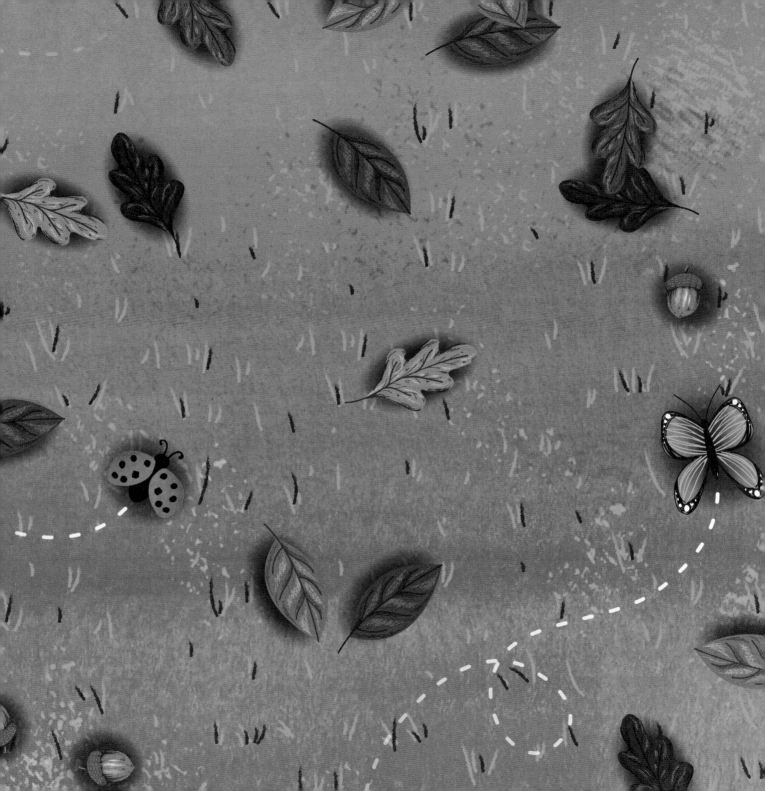

For Clark

First Published in 2021 by Blossom Spring Publishing
I'll Get You Home Copyright © 2021 Lauren Armstrong and Fay Cavagin
ISBN 978-1-8384972-7-9
E: admin@blossomspringpublishing.com
W: www.blossomspringpublishing.com

Lauren Armstrong and Fay Cavagin as the authors and Fiona Couling as the illustrator, have been asserted in accordance under the Copyright, Designs and Patents Act,1988.

I'll Get You Home

By Lauren Armstrong & Fay Cavagin

Illustrated by Fiona Couling

Night arrived and Little Mole popped up to wander free.
He ventured far and wide making friends and drinking tea.
But soon the bright sun began to rise over the forest floor.
"Oh dear I'm late, I must escape, I've never been this far before!"

Little Mole worried, "I can't smell my home!
I'm lost and scared and feel all alone.
My home feels like happiness, warmth and love.
Not cold and miserable with rain from above."

As a small tear rolled down his wet little cheek,
he heard something, a sound, a distant squeak.
"Who's there? Can you help? I can't find my house."
From under the leaves popped up a brown mouse.

The mouse gave a sigh, a peep and a squeak,
"Oh Little Mole... you're stood at a creek.
Let me describe what I can see,
I'll get you home, stick with me."

The mouse described the green, murky waters,
mossy rafts and huge rocky boulders.
Little Mole knew he had miles to go,
but now with a friend he wasn't so low.

The mole and mouse walked a bit further,
then above their heads they heard a murmur.
"Stop please! I need help! Can my voice be heard?"
Out from the trees swooped down a blue bird.

The bird came to the mole in the dark,
"Oh Little Mole... You're stood at a park.
Let me describe what I can see,
I'll get you home, stick with me."

The bird described rusty slides,
dangling swings and grass far and wide.
Little Mole knew he had miles to go,
but now with a friend he wasn't so low.

The mole, mouse and bird went on their way.
When all of a sudden, the mouse saw something sway.
"Please help! I've lost my home! It's near some rocks."
Out pounced the face of a sly looking fox.

The fox had a sniff and took a step near,
"Oh Little Mole... you have nothing to fear.
The burrows are close, I'll say what I see.
I'll get you home, stick with me."

The fox described muddy holes deep and dark.
He looked at the mole, whose eyes had a spark.
"I'm back! It's here! This is my house!
Thank you fox, bird and squeaky brown mouse!"

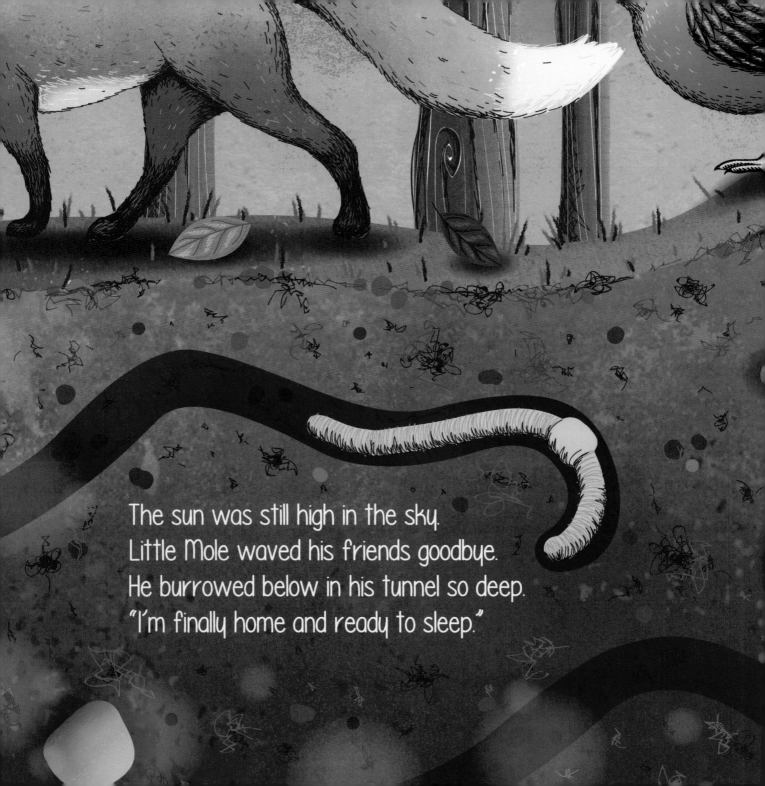

The sun was still high in the sky.
Little Mole waved his friends goodbye.
He burrowed below in his tunnel so deep.
"I'm finally home and ready to sleep."

www.blossomspringpublishing.com

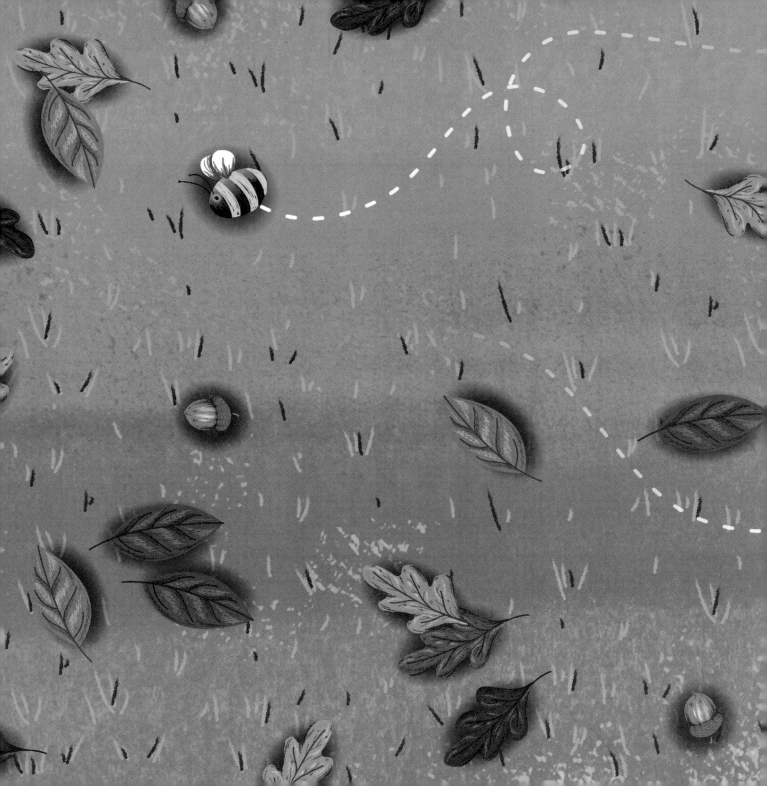

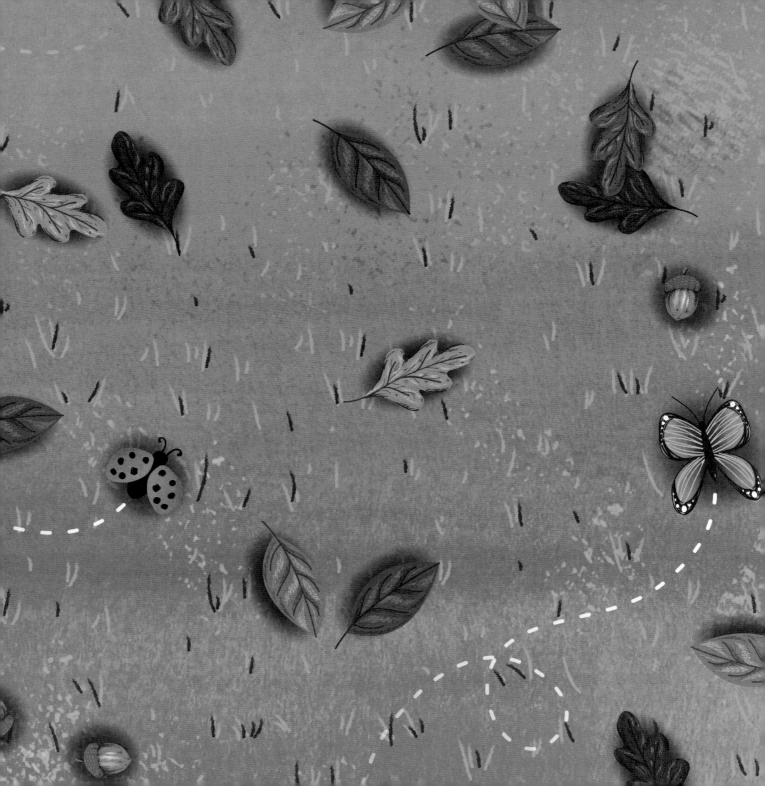

Printed in Great Britain
by Amazon